THE BOOK OF Mermaids

PATRICIA SAXTON

Shenanigan Books

for Carolyn

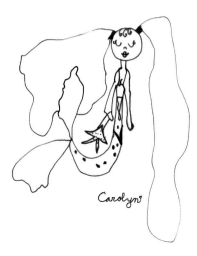

Printed in China

The type is set in Goudy, Kendo ITC, P22 Cezanne-Regular and Trajan.

The illustrations have been created using pencil, colored pencil, watercolor, marker and acrylics, with shadow accents created in Adobe Photoshop.

Library of Congress Control Number: 2005931590

ISBN: 978-0-9726614-6-1

THE BOOK OF Mermaids

table of contents

Mermaid LEGEND

Ben-Varry
Isle of Man

Ceasg
Scottish

Gwragedd, Annwn
Welsh

Hafgufa
Iceland

Havmand
Norwegian

Liban
Irish, sanctified

Loreli
German, Rhine

Makemind
Danish

Meerfrau
German

Melusine
Europe, double-tailed

Merrow
Irish

Merrymaid
Cornish

Morgens
British

Nakinneito
Finnish

Neck
Scandinavian

Ningyo
Japanese

Rusalki
Russian, Slavic

Mermaids Around The World

THROUGHOUT TIME, Mermaids have been seen all over the world. Some of us believe Mermaids are real – some don't. But whether or not you believe, and whether or not you have actually seen a Mermaid yourself, Mermaids have been the source of many a legend and countless tales.

Long, long, long ago, ancient cultures worshiped Mermaids as powerful gods. Hundreds of years later, when people began to explore more of the world, scores of Mermaid sightings were reported at sea and along the shores of mighty lakes. During this time, Mermaids were no longer considered religious figures, instead becoming creatures of awe, beauty and intrigue.

Some Mermaids were imagined to be cruel and bad-tempered. Others were thought to be kind. There were those who considered it unlucky to look upon Mermaids; others deemed it fortunate. Over time, a wealth of scholarly literature emerged, along with fantastic Mermaid paintings for all to see. Mermaids had become a part of our world.

To this day, people remain fascinated with Mermaid mystery, myth and fantasy. And Mermaids are almost always believed to have magical powers. Some even say that they may occasionally take on human form and walk among us ....

do you believe?

Where Mermaids Live

MERMAIDS usually live right where we'd expect them to – in the great seas and oceans. Here, with their fellow Merfolk, they live among schools of spectacular fish and rich, wondrous plant life. Mer-villages are generally situated in the most beautiful and secluded sections of the ocean, where colorful gardens thrive and magnificent sources of light radiate from the deep. Mainly near undersea caves and rock formations, their comfortable homes are well protected from intruders and potential enemies.

Occasionally, Mermaids vacation in very large lakes. Some stay longer, making a lake their home for a few years – but these are the quieter ones who prefer a fair amount of solitude. Lake living, while refreshing, doesn't offer the variety of food, entertainment or community found at sea. Merfolk tend to be social creatures, so after spending a couple of months in a lake region most find themselves inevitably drawn back to the salt, the sea, and the abundance of ocean culture.

CULTURE & Traditions

Home and Family

MERMAIDS ARE EXCEPTIONALLY family oriented. Loyalty and friendship are deeply valued. And they are quite serious in matters of the heart.

Mermaids marry and mate for life. Choosing partners is rather easy for some reason, and with few exceptions all Mermaids find their perfect partner. Marriages are traditionally held when the moon is full. Bride and groom take their wedding vows in the moon's bright glow, just below the water's surface. Then, in a beautiful dance ritual, they curl and entwine their fins and make a huge festive splash, tossing thousands of tiny, shiny sparkles out across the waves. Soon all the guests join in, celebrating with their own great big splashings at the moon.

A more uncommon marriage, though not an unthinkable one, can occur between a Mermaid and a human. The most famous marriage of this kind was portrayed in *The Little Mermaid*, a story originally written by Hans Christian Anderson. The story has been adapted over time, but the basic concept lives on!

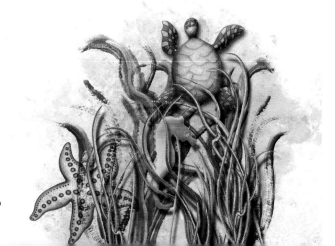

MERCHILDREN enjoy a happy, cheerful life, with loads of games to play and treasures to discover. They have endless fun investigating all the nooks and crannies in and around shipwrecks – and trying to figure out what some of the strange sunken objects might have been used for. Undersea caves are great for exploring too, and make perfect hiding spots when they play *Glide 'n Hide*.

Some other favorite games are *Wave*, which is similar to the human game of tag, and *Bubble Catch*, which is a bit like baseball except with fast-moving bubbles. *Show 'n Splash* is a game played to confuse humans – a pastime that Mermaids find hilarious. Another popular game is *Marco Polo*. This is a familiar human game too, but not many people know that it first originated among Mermaids. And not surprisingly, they love the all-time classic game *Diving for Treasure*.

Mer-babies are joyful little creatures who get lots and lots of cuddling. Cradled in giant clamshells upon thick cushions of velvety sea leaves, they like to play peek-a-boo with oysters. But their favorite thing to do is watch the older Mer-kids – and most of all, they like watching them make music. So, from a very young age the little ones are eager to learn to play their *own* musical instrument.

Most Mer-families also have fun frolicking with at least one friendly Mer-pet. The most common pets are turtles, starfish, seahorses, clownfish – and yes, dolphins!

Community

A MER-KING AND QUEEN preside together, with great kindness, over vast sections of the Merworld. Merfolk are very good-natured, so the breaking of any Mer-law is pretty rare. But when it happens, the wrongdoer loses privileges and is required to perform extra community work. The most harshly disciplined act is dishonesty, which can carry a punishment of temporary – or even permanent – exile.

Individual villages have a Mer-Lord or Mer-Lady watching over the safety and comfort of the villagers. Other prominent positions are held by the Mer-Scientist, the Mer-Mathematician, the Mer-Witch (or Wise Woman) and the Mer-Wizard. And *always* notably respected are the Mermaids. Not only are they beautiful, they are tremendous healers and are renowned for their marvelous magical powers. Enchanted water fairies are popular community members too, often spotted dancing among coral groves or sprinkling fairy dust in the gardens.

SCHOOL IS TAUGHT by the elder Merfolk. By the age of seven, Merchildren are quite knowledgeable in science, reading, writing and mythology, and are ready to begin advanced studies in fishology, mathematology, aquarionomy, and the art and philosophy of physics. Merchildren are so bright and creative that one day a week school gets "turned around," and the children teach the elders! All school sessions are held during the morning hours, after which *all* Merfolk go and play.

11

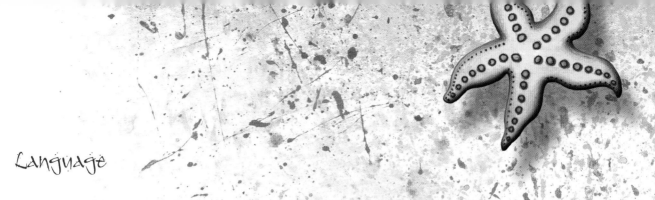

Language

MER-LANGUAGE IS UNIVERSAL among all Mermaids. A few of their common, everyday words have now been translated into the human language. Try them!

O-kee'-ya: hello

Jai-quay': good-bye, 'til next time

Flar'-sha: thank you

Ma-nee'-sa-may: a term for friend

See'-la: yes, and okay

Quid'-did: no

Na-nee-na-no'-kay: don't talk with your mouth full

Choo'-poo: how are you

Shay?: what? excuse me? pardon me

O'-loo: a blessing (or when someone sneezes)

Da-du': party

Mermaids have the ability to understand and communicate with other creatures. They can adapt their own speech and hearing to the style and frequency of each fish or mammal (including humans), and carry on a complete conversation. This amazing trait is just another sign of Mermaids' extremely high intelligence.

The Arts

MERMAIDS ADORE COLORFUL stories, lively conversations and just about every kind of art. All are encouraged to delve into whatever art form inspires them. Most villages have a performance theatre, several art galleries and at least one orchestra. It's also a neat fact that when an orchestra practices in a village garden, there is a flourish of luscious blooms.

Gardens are an important part of each village. Everyone shares equally in tending the gardens for their beauty as well as for food – even for growing artistic tools. Certain types of coral, for example, are prized for their brilliant inks. Specially grown seaweed is intertwined and prepared with flower oils, then layered and pressed to make scrolls for writing and waterpainting. Common seaweeds are finely shaven for stringing harps and guitars. Crab claws and small shells fertilize garden soils – and they're often used for maracas too. Abandoned turtle and stingray shells make excellent drums, and large triton shells have long been used as trumpets.

A large variety of shells and seaweeds are finely crafted into jewelry, hair ornaments, handbags, belts and oodles of decorative objects. It's pretty easy to see that shells and seaweed are essential elements in the Mermaid world!

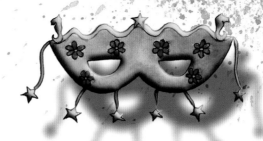

Holidays

INTRIGUINGLY, several Mer-holidays share a striking resemblance to human holidays. Here are a few:

MoonTide is a sacred and jubilant holiday observed during the last week of December. It's a time of gift-giving and good will – and it's a time that holds special excitement for children. Traditionally, Merchildren leave large clamshells beside their beds at night, and awaken to find them filled with delightful treasures!

Blossom Day is celebrated in early spring when the first undersea flowers bloom. Fish eggs are collected and colorfully decorated, honoring the season of new life. Merfolk feast, play games, and revel in the lush sculpture gardens that are specially set aside for meditation and giving thanks.

CoralStar marks the independence of Merfolk from the oppressive rule of the Bleerka Sea Tribe over 1000 years ago. The Bleerka were wicked, ruthless sea-warriors, who are now believed to be extinct. To celebrate their freedom, Mermaids weave brightly colored flags and parade them through villages every July 31st.

The Festival of Spirits takes place at the end of October. Lavish costumes are worn as Merfolk indulge in a full weekend of exceptional concerts and theatre. In addition, ceremonies are held to attract spiritual knowledge from Merfolk past. And it is well-known that spells cast at festival time can be tremendously powerful!

Jewel Time is an extravagant celebration of the arts that occurs every third year and lasts for three weeks. Great efforts go into preparation and sharing of the finest artistic talents from surrounding Mermaid communities. The Jewel Time holiday features outstanding storytelling, poetry readings, music, theatre, dance, fancy feasts, and competitive athletic games.

Jewel Time is dedicated to Shamanna, the legendary Mermaid Goddess recognized by the three magical pearls worn around her waist. It was known that Shamanna healed the sick with her beautiful songs, that her dance could move the seas, that her paintings delivered a lasting inner peace to those who looked upon them — and that her wit and lyrical laughter brought pure joy to hearts everywhere. As a tribute to Shamanna, Mermaids of today wear elaborate jewelry throughout the Jewel Time festivities.

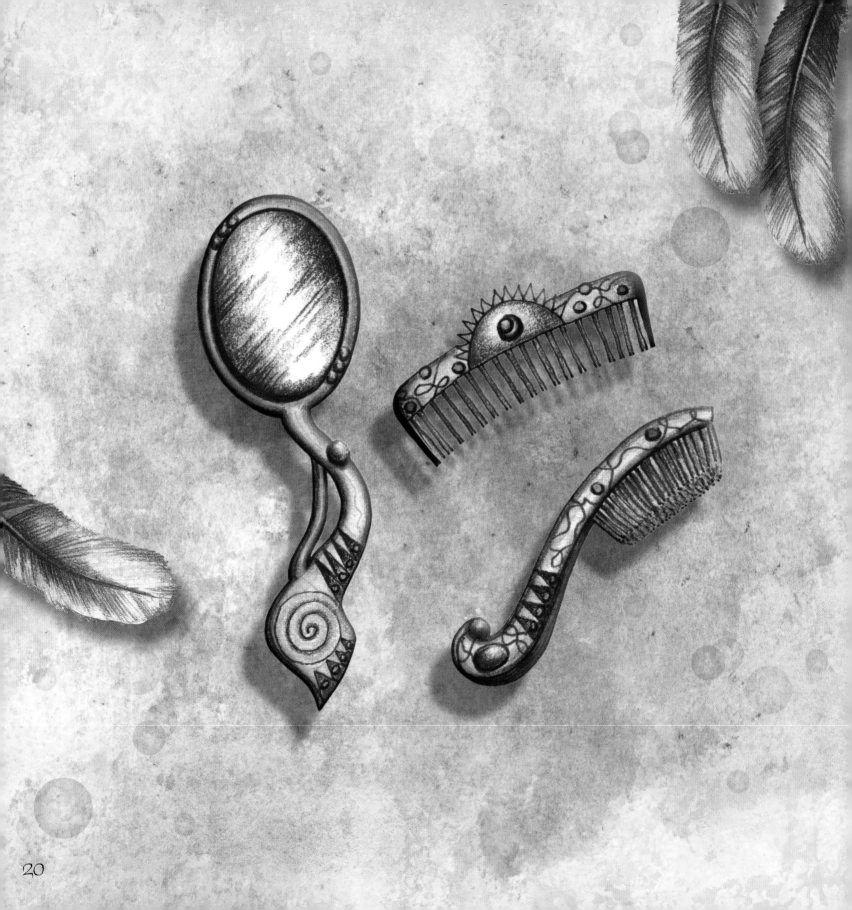

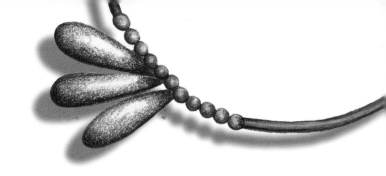

Mermaid MAGIC

Magical Secrets

KNOWN FOR THEIR CHARM and beauty, Mermaids do cherish their mirrors, combs and brushes. Often quite ornamental and exquisitely designed, these everyday items also serve as magical tools. By brushing their hair, Mermaids strengthen their magical powers ... and with a touch of beautifully scented oil, they weave secrets and spells into hair braids. Mermaids can also divine the future and unravel mysteries of the past by steadily gazing into a mirror.

Mermaids love, love, love to sing! And they sing extraordinarily well. But music is not only for pleasure, it is for magic making. With song, they can quiet a storm or stir up the seas into raging waves. With mesmerizing harp melodies they soothe and soften hurt or angry souls. With chants and chimes they magnify their psychic gifts, allowing them to find lost objects and move things at will. And during healing ceremonies, Mermaids combine hauntingly lovely chords and rhythms with the magical ingredients of plants, shells and sea stones.

PEARLS are another powerful, mystical tool. Holding a pearl over their own heart, many Mermaids can see into the bodies of others and diagnose almost any illness. Mixtures of pearls and blue sea stones are rubbed on the forehead to cure headaches, read minds and predict storms. Pearls worn on the left wrist bring true love and keep away quarreling.

QUITE MYSTERIOUSLY, Mermaids possess one of the world's most remarkable magical skills – the art of transformation – enabling them to transform into human bodies for several days at a time. Silver shells worn as a necklace let Mermaids travel between water and land. During the day, the necklace gathers and stores energy from the sun, allowing a Mermaid to breathe air for longer periods of time. Most Mermaids find it easiest to remain on land during the night, especially when the sky is clear and the moon is full. However, whether night or day, a Mermaid in human form will usually carry seagull feathers. These seemingly simple feathers are considered very protective and are often worn with jewelry or clothing to fend off possible evil.

Some Mermaids can also take on the form of a dolphin, a seagull or a swan, particularly in situations of danger. And the very, *very* powerful have been known to make themselves entirely invisible.

IN ALL THE MERWORLD, Mermaids are the only ones born with a deeply intuitive knowledge of ancient healing techniques – which makes them extraordinary healers. A lesser known secret is that on bright, starry nights, Mermaids love to go up to the ocean's surface and listen to the stars. Stars contain rare and marvelous wisdoms which are transferred to the attentive Mermaids.

Mermaids have a special relationship with starfish as well, and all Mermaids have a starfish friend they talk with. This is because starfish are thought to carry some of the same secrets held by the stars in the sky.

CLOTHING *& accessories*

Fashion

BEAUTY AND STYLE come naturally to Mermaids. As with most of their artistry, Mermaids approach fashion with a sense of fun and flair. But the business of making clothing is a serious craft.

Mermaid seamstresses make clothing in every possible color, texture and style. First, plants and minerals are mixed in precise measurements under specific temperatures to create color dyes for fine silks and yarns. Then fabrics are designed and intricately woven on huge undersea looms. Crushed shells, coral and stones are skillfully manipulated into a multitude of effects. These textural treatments are applied directly to finished cloth or blended into unfinished materials. Once all these preparations are complete, the careful work of stitching begins. It's also common for Mermaids to sew hats and bags to complement an outfit.

JEWELRY is an accessory no Mermaid goes without. Unless given as a gift, each piece of jewelry is usually made by the Mermaid who will wear it. This means that every piece has a distinct personality – and sometimes a bit of magic sprinkled in!

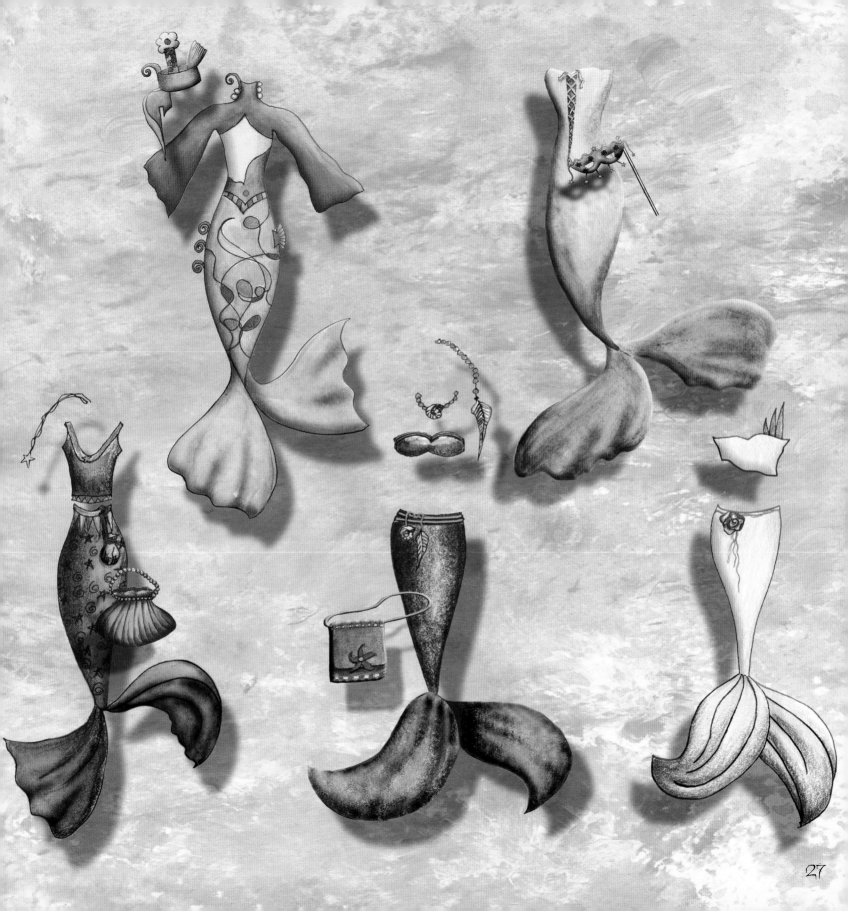

What's Your Style?

A MERMAID'S STYLE is a whole combination of things expressing individuality. It's in how they speak, how they work and play, and even how they treat others. Of course, it's found in fashion too. Sometimes a dash of color says it all – sometimes bold accessories show it best. But Mermaids understand that the *real* key to style isn't about their clothing. It's tucked inside a time-tested style tip that every Mermaid knows: if you keep the inside of yourself genuine and beautiful – and keep a happy heart – your own special beauty will shine throughout the sea.

If you were a Mermaid, what would your style say about you? Would your look be cute? Sophisticated? Glamorous? Casual? Elegant? Playful? Would you have fancy going-to-a-party clothes? Free-spirited artsy clothes? Maybe sporty play-in-the-waves clothes? Would you wear hats? Shells, feathers and bows in your hair? Would you be dripping in jewelry, or keep it simple? Would you dress your pet?

Maybe you'd be a Mermaid fashion designer; just think of all the amazing colors and designs you could use! Maybe you'd be a journalist or storyteller. Why not get out some paper and give it a try? Be creative – be imaginative – and have fun!

And if you're ever near the sea, take a good long look out across the waves. Take in the wonder of it all … and just maybe you'll see something that glimmers like a Mermaid.

Jai-quay!